The Legend of Good Women

Published by The Langley Press, 2023

To Michelle Caulkett

The Legend of Good Women

by

Geoffrey Chaucer

In a Modern English Version

by

Simon Webb

Contents

Al be hit / that he can nat wel endite
yet hath he made lewde folke delyte
To serve yow / in preysing of your name
he made the book / that hyght the hous of ffame
And eke the deeth of Blaunche the Duchesse
And the parlement of foules / as I gesse
Of Thebes / thogh the storye ys knowen lyte
And many an ympne for your halydayes
That highten balades roundels virelayes
And for to speke of other holynesse
he hath in prose translated Boece
And maade the lyfe also of seynt Cecile
he made also / gon ys a grete while
Origenes / vpon the Maudeleyne
hym oughte now / to have the lesse peyne
he hath maade many a lay / and many a thinge
Now as ye be a god / and eke a kynge
I your Alceste / whilom quene of Trace
I aske yow this man / ryght of your grace
That ye him never hurte in al his lyve
And he shal swerin to yow / and that blyve
he shal never more agilten in this wyse
But shal maken / as ye wol devyse
Of wommen trewe / in lovyng al hir lyfe
Wher so ye wol of mayden or of wyfe
And forthren yow / as muche as he mysseyde
Or in the Rose / or elles in Creseyde
The god of love / answerede hir anoon
Madame quod he / it is so long agoon
That I yow knewe / so charitable and trewe
That never yet / sin that the worlde was newe
To me ne fonde y better man than yee
If that ye wolde / save my degree
I may ne wol nat / werne your requeste
Al lyeth in yow / dooth wyth hym as yow liste
I al foryeve / withouten lenger space

Page from manuscript Fairfax 16

Introduction

For centuries, readers have been puzzled by the title Geoffrey Chaucer chose for his *Legend of Good Women*. At the heart of his poem are the stories of ten famous women from history, myth and legend, not all of whom can be described as good, at least not by the standards of the Christians of the Middle Ages. Several of the women had sex outside of marriage, and some committed suicide. Although the ancient Romans admired people who, under certain circumstances, chose to kill themselves, the Christian Church of Chaucer's time regarded suicide as a terrible sin. Medea, perhaps the worst of the women whose stories are re-told in the *Legend*, was a witch who killed her own brother, her children and her husband's second wife.

Was Chaucer being sarcastic when he labelled these characters 'good' women, or was he trying to make us see the good in them? Perhaps he was implying that women as a whole are such a bad bunch that the best of them are riddled with faults. If we opt for the last explanation, then *The Legend of Good Women* is a misogynist poem; but there is plenty of both external and internal evidence to suggest that the poet did not intend to write such a hateful work.

To begin with, some of the women in Chaucer's *Legend* are blameless, even positively virtuous. Hypsipyle, the unfortunate first wife of Jason, merely makes the mistake of marrying and having children by an unreliable man who runs off and leaves her to die of a broken heart. Although the aftermath of her rape is truly horrific, Philomela is only 'guilty' of having been raped and then telling everyone who the rapist was. Lucretia, who committed suicide after having been raped, was celebrated for centuries as a woman of outstanding courage and virtue.

In his Prologue to the *Legend*, Chaucer tells us that he was ordered by the god of love to write a series of stories about women who had been wronged by men. The god appeared to him in a dream, and set him his writing assignment as a penance, to make up for works he had already written, that tended to cast shade on women. These include his *Troilus and Criseyde*, where the heroine, Criseyde or Cressida, is unfaithful to her lover Troilus.

In his *Legend*, Chaucer could certainly have chosen to re-tell the stories of women whose lives were better-suited to the task he had in hand. Thisbe is not betrayed by her Pyramus at all, and Mark Antony does not exactly desert Cleopatra: in Chaucer's version, he kills himself because he has just lost a crucial battle.

Readers familiar with Shakespeare will already know all of the names in the paragraphs above. The Stratford man wrote plays about both Troilus and Cressida and Antony and Cleopatra, and included a version of the story of Pyramus and Thisbe in his *Midsummer Night's Dream*. In the *Dream*, the 'rude mechanicals', workmen of Athens, attempt to stage the story to play at the marriage celebrations of Theseus (who also features in Chaucer's *Legend*) and the Amazonian queen Hippolyta.

Shakespeare's poem *The Rape of Lucrece* re-tells the story of one of Chaucer's heroines in the *Legend*, and in *Coriolanus* we learn that the hero of the play fought, as a youngster, in the war that was provoked by Tarquin's rape of Lucrece. The plot of Shakespeare's *Titus Andronicus* is so similar to the legend of Philomela that the playwright felt obliged to reference that grisly narrative in his play. Chaucer's *Knight's Tale*, from his *Canterbury Tales*, is thought to be a recycled version of his lost *Palamon and Arcite*, referenced in the Prologue to the *Legend of Good Women*. The story was re-cast as a play, *The Two Noble Kinsmen*, by Shakespeare and John Fletcher.

Despite all of these Shakespearian connections, it is difficult to trace direct links between the fourteenth-century poet and Shakespeare, as we know that Shakespeare used earlier sources for these stories, some of which were also used by Chaucer himself. Whether or not the old narratives Chaucer included in his *Legend* suit his stated purpose – to write about wronged women – the fact that they were constantly re-used must say something about their inherent power.

The Prologue to Chaucer's poem, where we are told a fantastic tale of how the work came to be written, exists in two different forms, which the Victorian editor William Skeat called A and B. Skeat evidently preferred B, which he printed in full: A only appears in pieces in his edition of the *Legend*. In the following translation, I have followed Skeat's version B, which he derived mainly from Fairfax 16, a manuscript from the mid-fifteenth century. Bequeathed to the Bodleian Library in Oxford by the Parliamentary Civil War general Thomas Fairfax (1612-1671), Fairfax 16 includes not only a version of Chaucer's

Legend, but also other works by Chaucer, and by Chaucer's contemporaries John Lydgate and Thomas Hoccleve, as well as some anonymous pieces.

Chaucer speaks directly to us in his Prologue, but the picture he paints of himself is typically modest and self-deprecating. He tells us he is a bookworm, but assures us that he has very little skill as a writer: he hopes that the authors of his sources will help make his poem worthwhile.

Medieval authors were often very up-front about their sources: originality was not something they were aiming for. In a world where the vast majority of people were illiterate, and books had to be copied by hand, it was an achievement to be able to access a book, let alone read it; especially if it was in a foreign language. What Chaucer repeatedly tried to do throughout his writing career was to present old material in a fresh new way. As well as re-telling old tales, he also translated part of *The Romance of the Rose*, a thirteenth-century French poem that was one of the most celebrated works of the Middle Ages, and also *The Consolation of Philosophy* by Boethius, a celebrated Roman thinker of the sixth century CE.

Although the stories in his *Legend* are ultimately derived from ancient Greece and Rome, some of Chaucer's immediate sources are later – for instance he mentions Boccaccio, and Guido della Colonna, a thirteenth-century Italian author who wrote a version of the legend of the destruction of Troy. Using medieval sources was one way for Chaucer to put his classical material through the filter of the Middle Ages. His ancient Greek, Roman, Egyptian and even Babylonian characters tend to behave like European contemporaries of the poet. One way this shows up has to do with the medieval courtly love tradition, which dictated that lovers should pine away hopelessly for the objects of their devotion, fail to eat and sleep, and become withdrawn and depressed.

Women who became the focus of courtly lovers might be treated like remote goddesses – like Alcestis in the Prologue to the *Legend*, for instance. But as medieval European wives and daughters they could be regarded very much as second-class citizens, victims of the misogyny of the age. A younger contemporary of Chaucer's, the French-Italian writer Christine de Pizan, became so depressed by anti-feminist texts that she set out to write her own elaborate version of Chaucer's *Legend*, though it is likely that the Englishman's work was quite unknown to her. Her *Book of the City of Ladies*, completed shortly after Chaucer's death, looks at the lives of many females, including several of Chaucer's good women, such as Medea, Dido, Hypsipyle, Lucretia and Thisbe.

As well as full-length translations into his own Middle English (the English of the Middle Ages) Chaucer included translated excerpts from his sources in his *Legend* and other works. The poet was at home not only with English but also with French, Latin and Italian. This meant that, just for the *Legend*, he was able to consult the works of Virgil, Ovid, Boccaccio and Dante, among others. At the end of the Prologue, Chaucer 'hits the books' which, he tells us, are locked up in a chest at home:

And with that word my bokes gan I take,
And right thus on my Legend gan I make.

(lines 578-9)

11

As a bookworm, Chaucer uses his Prologue to the *Legend of Good Women* to remind us of the importance of books to allow us to know about things that we cannot experience directly. He begins with the example of heaven and hell: belief in these places (as well as, at this date, Purgatory) was essential for Western Christians, yet, as Chaucer reminds us, none of us has actually visited any of the lands of the afterlife.

The importance of belief in that which cannot be seen is emphasised in St Paul's second letter to the Corinthians, which readers can find in the New Testament. Paul speaks for his fellow-Christians when he says 'we look not at the things which are seen, but at the things which are not seen: for the things which are seen are temporal; but the things which are not seen are eternal' (2 Cor. 4:18, KJV).

Although it has pretty much always been acknowledged as a genuine work by Chaucer, his *Legend of Good Women* has until recently been almost as well-hidden as Paul's eternal 'things which are not seen'. In *The Legend of the Legend of Good Women*, an article published in *The Chaucer Review* in 1966 (Vol. 1, No. 2, pp. 110-133) Robert Worth Frank pointed out that the *Legend* was only printed in full in editions of the complete works of Chaucer, and that it tended to be neglected in works about Chaucer's output.

In 2023, I have found it easier to find books *about* the *Legend* than a modern stand-alone edition or translation. In fact the last useable edition I have been able to find is Skeat's, from 1889. Modern books *about* the *Legend* include Lucy M. Allen-Goss's 2020 *Female Desire in Chaucer's Legend of Good Women*, *Chaucer's Legendary Good Women* by Florence Percival (1998) and Sheila Delany's 1994 book *The Naked Text: Chaucer's Legend of Good Women*. The reader will notice that all three of these were written by women: as Delany notes, this long-neglected text is of particular interest for students of gender studies and related subjects.

The authors of modern books and articles about the *Legend* have tended to consult versions of the poem printed in, for instance, the latest *Riverside Chaucer*, a hefty but indispensable tome comprising over thirteen hundred pages, the latest edition of which was published by Oxford in 2008. Skeat's much earlier attempt at a complete works, garnished with extensive additional material, filled several separate volumes.

The fact that, in his Prologue, Chaucer in effect accuses himself of misogyny, and sets out to correct his fault by writing, makes the text a natural reference-point for medieval attitudes to women. That the poet seems to deliberately fail to make the women he writes about appear as total paragons just adds to the interest of his poem as a double-edged sword deployed in the 'battle of the sexes'. Whose side is Chaucer on?

It is thought that Chaucer wrote his *Legend*, which is unfinished, shortly before he started on his *Canterbury Tales*, which were also left incomplete at the time of his death in 1400. The *Tales* tend to overshadow the poet's earlier works, although many of them, particularly his 'love visions', are of enduring value. These are dream poems on the theme of love, and the *Legend of Good Women* is usually counted among them. The others, *The Book of the Duchess*, *The Parliament of Fowls* and the *House of Fame* (the last of which Chaucer also failed to finish) are all available in modern English versions from the Langley Press. Like the *Legend*, these are poems that feature dreams, in which the poet himself appears. They tackle such themes as the nature of love, the truth about grief and loss, and the value of fame.

The *Legend* is the only one of the love visions that tells a series of stories, though the others have references to old stories embedded in them like jewels in a gold necklace. Compilations of stories were, however, popular in Chaucer's time, especially collections of hagiographies, or saints' lives. Christine de Pizan's city of ladies provides accommodation for a number of female saints from the Christian tradition.

Chaucer's *Canterbury Tales* is of course a set of inter-connected stories, and some of the poet's favourite sources followed a similar pattern. These included the *Decameron* of Boccaccio and the *Heroides* of Ovid. The latter was particularly useful to Chaucer when he was writing his tales of women who had had a hard time of it because of men. The *Heroides* are poetic letters supposedly sent by heroines like Dido and Medea to the men who had wronged them. In his *Legend*, Chaucer often includes translated extracts from Ovid's letters in his stories of good women.

Although Chaucer had access to (or knowledge of) some excellent sources, some of his accounts in the *Legend* differ wildly from what readers might have encountered elsewhere. The poet excludes any mention of Cleopatra's affair with Julius Caesar, and an innocent reader might come away from this legend thinking that Mark Antony was the first official visitor the Romans ever sent to Egypt. The Greek historian Plutarch tells us that Antony botched a suicide attempt after he heard that Cleopatra had killed herself (she had not). Chaucer's Antony kills himself after he loses the Battle of Actium. Chaucer also gives an account of the Egyptian queen's subsequent suicide which Skeat is right to describe as 'very peculiar'.

The source of this particular version of the death of Cleopatra is a little mysterious, but much of Chaucer's other content in the *Legend* can be explained. I hope that the glossary of names and places at the end of this book will help readers understand unfamiliar references.

The Legend of Good Women

Prologue

I have heard it said a thousand times, that there is joy in heaven, and pain in hell. I'm sure it's true, but I'm also sure that there is nobody living in this whole country who has been in either heaven or hell. The only way that anyone can find out about these places is by hearsay, or by reading something. No man can prove the existence of either heaven or hell from personal experience. But, God forbid that men should only believe what they have seen with their own eyes! They should not believe that anything is a lie, just because they have not seen it or done it themselves. God knows that nothing is less true just because nobody can see it. Even Bernard the monk didn't see everything, by God!

For this reason, we must use any books that we can find, to learn about things that happened long ago. And we should give credence to the doctrines of the wise old authors, to the best of our ability, when they tell good old tales, about holiness, and kingdoms, and victories, and love, and hate, and other things that I won't mention. If there were no old books like these, the key of remembrance would be lost, which means that we should honour and believe these volumes, especially where we can find no proof outside their pages.

As for myself, I know very little, but I love to read books, and I believe what I read in them and have faith in what they say. In fact, I reverence them so much, and with such a full heart, that there is no kind of fun that can lure me away from my books, unless, occasionally, on a holiday. Certainly, when the month of May arrives, and I hear the birds singing, and the flowers start to pop up, then I say farewell to my book and my devotion!

To my mind, the best of all the flowers in the meadow are those white and red flowers, which men in our town call 'daisies'. As I've said before, I love them so much that as soon as day dawns I'm up and walking in the meadow, to see these flowers spread out in the early-morning sun. When I see that blissful sight, all my sorrows seem to soften. I am so glad to be in the presence of this flower that I show it all kinds of reverence.

She is the flower of flowers, full of virtue and honour, always fair and fresh-coloured. I love her with a love that is always fresh, and I always will love her, until my heart stops beating. I do not need to swear – I will not lie – nobody's love has ever been so warm.

When it gets towards evening, and the sun moves into the west, I run out to watch the daisy preparing to sleep – she hates the darkness, but she boldly shows her face to the bright sun, when she opens herself. Oh, I wish I had enough English to give this flower her due, either in prose or rhyme! I hope I can rely on help from the clever and the mighty, especially from you lovers! Use your feelings and be diligent to help me in my work, whether you belong to the flower or the leaf! I know only too well how you lovers have got there before me, and harvested the crop, and taken away the corn. I'm a johnny-come-lately; I look around and am glad to get a few left-over ears, or a good word or two, that have been left behind. I hope that the old authors will not be impatient with me if I often re-tell the tales contained in their fresh songs.

I serve the flower as well as I can, given my strength and my brains. She is clearness and the true light that leads me through this dark world. The heart that beats in my sad breast dreads you, and loves you so painfully that you are truly the mistress of my mind, and I am nothing. My work and words are bound to you, so that I am like your harp, and with your fingering you can play any tune on my heart, either sad or merry. Be my guide and my sovereign lady: I call on you as I would call on a god that has come down to earth. I need your help with this work, and with all the sorrows that I suffer.

But why did I write about believing old stories, and revering them, and that men should believe more things than they can prove, or see with their own eyes? I will explain that in the right place: I cannot write about everything all at once.

Now, my restless spirit, that always pushes me to see this young, fresh-coloured flower, made my desire burn so hot that I can still feel it in my heart. It made me rise before dawn, this being the first day of May, to be present at the resurrection of this flower with a respectful, devoted heart. Then it was that the flower opened to the sun; a red morning sun that lodged in the breast of the animal that stole away Agenor's daughter.

The meadow was embroidered all over with sweet flowers. The odour was such that it cannot be compared to that of any one perfumed gum, or herb, or tree. The scent of the meadow was better than all these, and it exceeded all flowers in beauty. It was as if the earth had forgotten the sorry state he had been in all through the winter, that had left him naked and desperate. Then he had been wounded by the sword of bitter cold, but now the temperate sun undid all that harm, and clothed his nakedness anew.

Those little birds that had escaped the panther and the fowler's net loved the new season. In winter, the fowler had terrified them and killed their chicks, but now the birds thought it did them good to sing about him. In their song, they cast shade on him, calling him a foul, greedy churl, who had betrayed them with his sophistry. They sang, 'The fowler we defy, and all his craftiness!'

Some of the birds sang love-songs in clear voices: these were a joy to hear. In some of their songs, the birds praised and worshipped their mates. In other songs, they praised Saint Valentine, for the sake of the new summer, as they perched on branches laden with soft blossoms. 'Blessed be Saint Valentine,' they sang, 'for on this day I choose you to be mine, without repenting, my sweetheart!' With that, they touched beaks, honouring and showing obedience to love, and did other things that belong to love and nature (you can interpret that as you like, it's up to you).

Those who had been unkind (as small birds will, for the sake of variety) asked to be forgiven, and sang songs about how remorseful they were. They swore on the blossoms to be faithful in future, so that their mates would feel sorry for them. In the end, they came to an agreement. For a while, there was tension, but the power of pity, mercy, innocence and courtesy led to forgiveness. Now, I am not saying that innocence is folly, or pity false. Ethic tells us that 'virtue is the mean' – that is what I am trying to say. And so the birds, without any malice, followed love's course, and put aside the vice of hate. They sang together, 'Welcome, summer, our lord and governor!'

While the birds sang, Zephirus and Flora breathed gently on the flowers with their sweet breaths, and made them open their petals as if they were the gods and goddesses of the flowery meadow. In fact it was all so beautiful that I thought that I could happily live for ever in that place, in the jolly month of May, and go without food and drink, and even without sleep.

Soon I began to sink down, and ended up lying on my side, propped up on my elbow. To be honest, I planned to spend the whole long day right there, doing nothing but looking at the daisy. It is quite right that men call this flower the 'daisy', as it is truly 'the eye of the day', the empress and flower of all flowers. I wish her all good things, and I wish the same for all who love flowers.

You should not suppose that I intend to praise the flower more than the leaf, any more than I would praise the sheaf more warmly than the corn itself. I prefer neither the one nor the other. I am not concerned about who serves the leaf, and who the flower, or who enjoys their service most. The work I have in hand has quite a different tone: the story is old, and pre-dates such things.

When the sun began to set in the west, and the flower began to close itself and go to sleep, for fear of the dark night that was coming on, then I hurried home to my own house. There, I gave order that my couch should be set up in my little grassy garden, because of the sweetness of the new summer, and I told them to strew my bed with flowers. There I lay down, closed my eyes, and fell asleep after an hour or two, and dreamed that I had returned to the meadow, to seek the flower that I so feared and loved.

There I saw the god of love, hand-in-hand with a queen, far off, walking toward me across the meadow. She was dressed in a royal green robe, and her hair was covered with a golden net. A white crown with small petals all round sat on top of the gold net, so that, honestly, it looked just like a daisy with its little white leaves. The crown was fashioned from a single piece of white orient pearl: surrounding the gold net and set above her green dress, it made her look just like a daisy.

The god of love himself wore a silk robe embroidered with green plants and rose-leaves, the freshest there had ever been since the beginning of the world. His hair looked gilded, and was crowned with the sun, not a heavy gold crown. His face shone so brightly that I could hardly bear to look at it. In his hands he carried two flaming arrows, as red as glowing coals, and I saw his wings spread out like the wings of an angel.

Men say that love is blind, but I am sure he saw me: he glared at me very sternly, so that, as he looked at me, my heart went cold. But to turn again to the queen he held by the hand, crowned in white and clothed in green, she was so womanly, and benign, and meek, that you could search over the whole world and never find half such beauty, at least not in a mortal creature. And so I will sing this song in her praise:

Balade

Hide, Absalom, your tresses of bright gold;
And Esther, shield your meekness for a while;
Fair Jonathan, put all your charms on hold;
Penelope, and Marcia, Cato's wife,

Do not assert your faithful wifehood now;
Hide all your charms, Isolde and Elaine,
My lady comes, to put you all to shame.

Lavinia, hide your looks from all the world,
And fair Lucrece, of Rome the noble boast,
Polixena, whose tragic fate unfurled
And Cleopatra, passionate and fine,
All hide your loving truth and your renown,
And Thisbe, also, for whom love brought pain,
My lady comes, to put you all to shame.

Hero, Dido, Laodamia, all of you,
And Phyllis, hanging for Demophoön,
And Canace, with her beauty pure and true,
Hypsipyle, betrayed and left to pine,
No, none of you should boast or make a sound;
Hypermnestra, Ariadne, lame;
My lady comes, to put you all to shame.

As I have said before, this balade should certainly be sung
whenever my lady appears, as none of the above-named ladies
is worthy to stand alongside her. She outshines everything, as
the sun will outshine a fire. She is so beautiful, so good, so
debonair! I pray to God that she will always meet with good
fortune. If it had not been for the comfort she brought me just
by being present, I would have been defenceless, and would

have been killed by Love's words and by his deadly glare (I will tell you about this later).

On the green behind the god of love there appeared nineteen ladies, royally dressed, walking at an easy pace. After them came so many women that I guess a third or fourth part of all the people who had ever lived since the time of Adam were there. And all of these women had been true in love.

It may or may not have been a wonderful thing, but as soon as these women spotted the daisy, they deliberately stopped, knelt down and sang with one voice, 'Health and honour to truth in womanhood, and to this flower who symbolises what we are! Her crown is our witness!'

With that word, they softly sat down in a wide circle. First the god of love sat down with his queen, in her green robe and white crown, then all the rest, courteously, according to their status. Silence reigned over the whole scene, for a furlong all round. Meanwhile, I continued to kneel by my flower, as still as a stone, wondering why all these people had appeared.

At last, the god of love looked at me again, and asked, 'Who is that kneeling there?' As soon as I heard his question, I answered, 'Sir, it's me,' and came closer to him, and saluted him.

'What are you doing so near my flower? How can you be so bold?' he asked then. 'I'd rather see a worm kneeling near my flower, than you.'

'But why sir,' I asked, 'if you don't mind my asking?'

'Because it has nothing to do with you,' he answered. 'It is my relic, dignified and delightful, and you are my enemy. You make war against my people, and misrepresent my faithful old servants. You hinder them with your translations, and discourage them, and tell them that it is folly to serve love! You cannot deny it, your offence is there for all to see! It needs no explanation – you have translated *The Romance of the Rose*, which is heresy against my law – and you make wise people pull away from me. You also said what you liked about Criseyde, and what you said made men trust women less, even women who are as true as steel.

'Before you answer,' he went on, 'think hard. I know that many others have turned against me, as you have, but by Venus my mother, if you live, you will bitterly repent your actions, and everyone will see it!'

'My god,' said the lady in the green robe, 'you must be courteous enough to listen to him, if he can make any reply to all that you have said to him. A god should not be upset – you should be calm, gracious and merciful. If you were not one of those gods who knows everything, I'd tell you what might happen. This man may have been falsely accused, and in that case you would have to acquit him. In your court you have many flatterers, tattlers and accusers, who pipe tunes into your ears. What they tell you is born out of their own imaginations. They speak out of envy, and to make you their friend – that's all they want. Envy is always hanging around the court, night and day, like a laundress, always in Caesar's house, as Dante says. And many in the court are just there to make themselves rich.

'It may be,' she went on, 'that this man is so stupid that he cannot even recognise that he has done anything wrong. He makes things, and he may not understand his raw materials. It is also possible that he was asked by someone else to write the two things you have mentioned, and dared not refuse. He may also be very sorry for what he has done already. And we know that he has not translated what old writers have written against love, and tried to pass it off as his own original work.

'This is the sort of thing that a righteous ruler should keep in mind,' the lady added. 'That way, he will not end up like one of the lords of Lombardy, who excel only in their tyranny. Anyone who is a lord by nature should not be a cruel tyrant, like a tax-collector, who does all the harm he can. He should think of his subjects as men who owe him allegiance, as treasures that he owns, like gold in a chest. This is what the philosophers tell us – a king must be sure to be just in his dealings with his people – that is his job.

'He should also maintain his lords in their positions, by rewarding, honouring and treasuring them, for they are like demi-gods in this world. But all the same, he must do right to both rich and poor, however these classes of people may differ from one another. He must show compassion to the poor, and act like a lion! When a fly pesters a lion, or even bites him, he brushes it away with his tail: the lion is too noble to kill a fly, as dogs and other animals do. Noble hearts should show restraint, and judge everything even-handedly, and reward people when they deserve it.

'It is not lordly to condemn a man without first hearing him out: that is a nasty thing for a lord to do. And if a man can offer no excuse for his wrong-doing, but feels remorse and begs for mercy, and offers himself up for judgement in nothing but a bare shirt, then a god should weigh up his case, quickly and fairly. This man has done nothing deserving of a death sentence, so you should be merciful. Relent, and turn your anger down a notch! The man has used his learning to serve you, and has worked to further your law.

'We all know he is not a good author, but he has encouraged common people to delight in serving you, and praising your name. He wrote a book called *The House of Fame*, and also *The Death of Blanche the Duchess* and *The Parliament of*

Fowls. I guess he also wrote about how love affected Palamon and Arcite, although that piece is little-known. He has also written hymns for days that are sacred to you, in the form of balades, roundels and virelays, and, in the way of holiness, he has also translated Boethius, and written a Life of St Cecilia. A long time ago, he also translated Origen's homily about Mary Magdalene. Really, on the basis of everything he has written, you should not give this man too hard a time.

'I address you as both a god and a king,' she continued. 'I, your Alcestis, who was once queen of Thrace, ask you, by your grace, not to hurt this man, for the rest of his life. In return, he will happily swear to you that he will never offend against you again. Instead, he will write about women who were always faithful in love. You yourself can choose the women: they can be either wives or virgins. In this way, the writer will advance your banner, to make up for his ill-judged *Rose* and *Cressida*.'

The god of love quickly answered, 'Madam, I have long known you to be truthful and charitable. In fact, I have never found anyone better than you, since the beginning of the world. I owe it to my position to grant your request: it's up to you, do what you like with him. For myself, I have forgiven him. If anyone gives you a gift, or does you a favour, these things are better if they are done or given at the right time. Lady, you should decide what *you* want to do with him. As for you,' he said, turning to me, 'you should thank my lady here.'

I got up, and then knelt down. 'Madam,' I said, 'may the god above reward you for making the god of love forget his wrath and forgive me. I hope that he will grant me a long enough life to be able to understand what you are, now that you have helped me. But truly, I never set out to do anything wrong, or to trespass against love. An honest man should not be counted a thief, and a true lover should not be blamed for writing about people who were dishonest in love. True lovers should be on my side, *because* I wrote about Cressida and the Rose. Whatever my sources said, my intention was to promote truth in love, and to cherish it, and to use examples to discourage people from following falsehood and vice. That was what I meant to do.'

Alcestis answered, 'That's enough of that. You need to learn that you cannot debate with Love himself about right and wrong. You have been forgiven; don't push it! Now I will tell you what penance you must do, to make up for your crime. Understand this: every year for the rest of your life, you must put aside most of your time to write glorious legends of good women, either wives or virgins. These women must all have been true in love – you must also include accounts of the faithless men who betrayed them. Frankly, some of these men spent their lives trying to see how many women they could humiliate – it was like a game to them.

'Let's face it, you don't look like a lover,' the lady continued, 'but you should speak well of love, in this work I command you to complete for me. So there you are – that is your penance. I will pray to the god of love,' she added, 'to order his own servants to help you in your task, and reward you. So go now,' she concluded, 'the penance is not too heavy. And when you have finished your book, you must give it to the queen, either at Sheen or at Eltham.'

At this, the god of love smiled and asked me, 'Do you know of any other woman; virgin, wife, queen or countess, or whatever, who would give you such a light punishment, when you deserve far worse? But pity always flows through gentle hearts, as you can see – she is what she is.'

'Oh sir, I can see that she is good,' I said.

'That is a true story, by my hood,' Love replied, 'and something that you should remember, if you have any sense. You have a book, haven't you,' he went on, 'at home in a chest, about the good Alcestis, who was turned into a daisy? She chose to die and go to hell in her husband's place, and Hercules brought her out of hell back into the light?'

'Yes!' I said; 'now I remember who she is! Is this really the good Alcestis, the daisy, that soothes my heart? I can sense her goodness now: it followed her from life into death. Her kindness to me doubles her renown! Now she has rewarded me for the love I feel for her flower, the daisy. It is no wonder that Jove turned her into a star: Agathon tells us this. I see now that her white crown is a symbol: she has as many virtues as she has petals on her crown. In remembrance of her, Cybele gave the daisy a white crown, and Mars added red instead of rubies.'

At this, the queen blushed, to be praised so much in her own hearing. Love turned to me and said, 'You made a big mistake when you wrote your balade, 'Hide, Absalon your tresses'. You forgot to include Alcestis here, although you owe her so much. She is also the very calendar for women that want to be lovers. She taught the whole art of fine loving, including how to live as a good wife, without over-stepping the bounds. You were evidently asleep when you wrote that, moron! You can make up for your mistake by including Alcestis among your good women, after you have written about the others. So fare you well – I have no more orders for you!

'But before I go, I will tell you this much: no true lover can ever be sent to hell. And these ladies sitting in a row are the ladies in your balade, if you can recognise them. You can find them all in your books: put them in your legend, and keep them in mind, if you can find out about them. Here there are twenty thousand more sitting around – all of them good women, who were true in love, whatever happened. You can rhyme about them as well, if you like. I must go home to Paradise with all this company; the sun is moving west. There I will always serve the fresh daisy.

'I command that you start your legends with Cleopatra: in that way, you will win my love. I want to see if there is any man who has suffered pain for love like hers. I know you can't write rhymes about everyone, like lovers used to do: it would be too long to listen to, or read. I'll be happy if you just cover the main points of these women's stories – if you are telling lots of tales, make them all short.'

At that, I went to my books, and began to write my Legend.

Cleopatra

After the death of Ptolemy, who ruled the whole of Egypt, his queen Cleopatra became sole monarch, until the Romans sent a senator, whose job it was to conquer kingdoms for Rome. The Romans were always doing this: they planned to take over the whole world. The name of this senator was Antony: Fortune had decided that he should come to grief and be a rebel against Rome itself.

Antony was married to Caesar's sister, but he left her in the lurch, without even telling her that he was leaving her, to go running after a new wife. This made for bad blood between himself, and Rome and Caesar.

Nevertheless, to be honest, this same senator was a worthy, gentle warrior, and his death was a great loss. But love for Cleopatra had driven him mad, and bound him so tightly in his cord that he thought the whole world was worthless. He reckoned that the only thing worth doing was to love and serve Cleopatra: he didn't even care if he died in battle defending her and hers.

This noble queen loved her knight, not without cause. He was so chivalrous and, if the books don't lie, he was so good-looking, genteel, wise and hardy that he deserved love from any woman alive. As for herself, she was as fair as a May rose: in short, she was soon his wife, and could do what she liked with him.

Since I have agreed to write a lot of stories, I will not bother to describe their wedding-feast. It would take too long, and I might then neglect to do justice to something really important. No, I will skip ahead to the important bits, and drop everything else.

So, Octavian was mad about Antony's behaviour, and put together an army to go all-out for his destruction. His host was made up of stout Romans, as cruel as lions. They got into their ships, and there I'll leave them. Antony knew what was going on, and did not fail to meet these Romans in battle. He took advice, and he and his wife took to their ships without delay. Soon they encountered the Romans at sea: the trumpet sounded, and there was much shouting – and shooting. Everybody fought hard: the great guns were brought into play, and the battle truly kicked off. Huge stones rained down, and grapnels were hooked round the ships' cables. Shearing-hooks were used to cut the enemy's ropes, and the pole-axes were swinging.

One man tried to hide behind the mast, but he was driven out and forced to jump over-board. Men stabbed each other with their spears' points, and some ripped sails with hooks like scythes. Some brought water for the wounded, and tried to cheer them up: others poured peas over the enemy's hatches, to make them slippery. Pots of lime were brought out, and thus they fought all day. But everything must end eventually: Antony was beaten, and he and his followers were put to flight.

The queen also ran away from the battle with its harsh blows, which had been as thick as hail. It is no wonder that she could not endure it. When Antony saw her purple sails receding in the distance, he cursed the day that he was born, and cried, 'My reputation is in tatters!' Despair made him lose his wits, and he stabbed himself in the heart. Cleopatra could get no mercy from Caesar, and so she fled back to Egypt out of fear and desperation.

But listen to this, if you want to hear about kindness! You men, who swear that you will die if your lady is angry with you! Here you will see a truthful woman! This Cleopatra was so devastated, that nobody could describe her state of mind. In the morning she stirred herself and had her workmen make a shrine, with all the rubies and fine stones of Egypt. She filled the shrine with spices, and had Antony's body embalmed. She shut up his corpse in the shrine, and dug a grave next to it.

This she filled with all the snakes she could find, then said, 'My love, my sorrowful heart obeyed you so completely, from that blissful time when I promised to be yours, and only yours. I mean you, Antony my knight! Day or night, you were never out of my mind, for good or bad, even when I was dancing. I promised myself that I would recompense your love, for good or bad, with my last ounce of strength. Then I knew that I would be a perfect wife, because my feelings would never change, whether I lived or died. I will keep that promise,' she went on, 'and everyone will see that there was never a truer queen in love.'

With that, she threw herself, naked, among the serpents in the pit: that was where she chose to be buried. The adders began to sting, but she died cheerfully, for love of her dear Antony. I'm not making this up – it's history!

And I pray to God that until I find a man so true and constant that he would kill himself like that for love, our heads never ache!

Thisbe

This story happened in Babylon, the town that Queen Semiramis fortified by surrounding it with ditches, and a wall of well-baked tiles. Once, in this noble town, lived two famous lords, whose houses were so close together that only a stone wall stood between them (this often happens in big towns). Now, one of these lords had a son, who was considered the lustiest in the town. The other lord had a daughter, the fairest woman in the east.

The son and daughter only came to know about each other thanks to their gossiping female neighbours, because in that country virgins were kept under tight control, for fear that they might do something stupid. Naso tells us that the young man was called Pyramus, and the girl, Thisbe. As they grew older, they began to fall in love, and in fact both were of an age to be married, but their fathers would not assent to this. Their love burned strongly, and nobody they knew could change their minds. Sometimes they were able to meet secretly, and discuss their love, but this just made their passion hotter. If a love is frustrated, it just becomes ten times more crazy.

Now, the wall that stood between the two lovers had been split from top to bottom, right to its foundation, for many years, but the cleft was so narrow that it was hard to see. But of course, the lovers spotted it! They were the first to discover the crack, and they spoke softly through it, as if they were at confession. Whenever they dared, they would go to the crack, and tell each other of their woeful love. Each stood on their own side of the wall, and listened for the sweet sound of each others' voices. In this way, they deceived those who watched over them.

Every day, they would threaten this wall, and wished to God that it would fall down. 'You wicked wall!' they would cry, 'out of spite, you have ruined everything! Why don't you split, or fall into two pieces? Or if not, why won't you let us meet just once, or let us kiss? Then we would feel better! I suppose we should be grateful to you though, for letting our words go through your stone and lime. I *suppose* we should be pleased with you.'

When they had spoken these idle words, they would try to kiss through the wall, but only kissed the cold wall itself. Then they would leave off for the day. They met like this late in the evening, or very early in the morning, so that they would not be observed. They carried on like this for a long time, but one morning, when Phoebus became visible, and Aurora's beams had dried up the dew that lay on the plants, Pyramus and Thisbe met again at the crack in their wall.

This time they promised each other that that very night they would slip their guards, steal away from their homes and flee the city. Because there was so much space in the countryside, they thought it best to meet at a particular place at a particular time. They agreed to meet at the grave of Ninus, which lay under a tree by a well (these old pagans who worshipped idols were often buried out in the fields). The lovers quickly agreed on all this, and, in short, found the rest of the day very long; but at last the sun went under the sea.

Thisbe loved Pyramus so much, and was so desperate to see him, that as soon as the time had come, she stole away into the night, her face wrapped up in a wimple. To keep her promise, she forsook all her family and friends – if only women would trust men like this when they knew them well enough!

Love had made her brave, and she made good time to the tree where they were to meet. There she was about to sit down by the well, when a wild lioness came out of the wood. The lioness's mouth was bloody because she had just killed some other beast, and she headed straight for the well to get a drink. At this, Thisbe started up, terrified, and dashed into a nearby cave. She had been able to see the lioness by the light of the moon. As she ran, her wimple came off and fell to the ground: Thisbe was so scared, and pleased to escape, she didn't even notice it. She sat very still in the cave, and outside it grew darker and darker.

When the lioness had drunk her fill, she began to stalk round and round the well, and found Thisbe's wimple. She tore it to pieces with her bloody teeth, then, when she was finished, she stole back into the wood. At last, Pyramus arrived, late, alas, having spent far too long at home. The moon shone brightly, and he could see everything. As he sped through the wood, he naturally looked around, and as he looked down, he saw the lionesses' large paw-prints in the sand. His heart trembled, he went pale and his hair stood on end. As he came upon the torn wimple, he cried out, 'Alas! The day that I was born! This night will kill us both! I cannot ask mercy of Thisbe, because it is I who has killed her, by forcing her to come here! What was I thinking? To ask her to come here, at night, to place her in danger, then turn up late? I should have been here ages ago! Whatever lion lives in this forest, he is welcome to tear me to pieces, and any other wild beast is welcome to gnaw on my heart!'

With these words, he approached the wimple, kissed it all over and wept on it. 'Wimple,' he said, 'there is only one way. Now you will taste my blood, as well as Thisbe's!' and with that he stabbed himself in the heart. His blood spurted out as thick as the water from a broken conduit.

Now Thisbe knew nothing of this: she was huddled up in fear, and thought, 'If my Pyramus turns up to find that I am not here, he may think I have been unkind and stood him up.' So she came out of her cave and looked around for him, both with her eyes and with her heart.

'I will explain to him about the lioness, and how much I feared her,' she thought, 'and how I hid away.' But at last she found her lover, covered in blood, beating his heels on the ground. She started back, and her heart began to beat like the waves of the sea. She grew as pale as box-wood, and very quickly assured herself that yes, it was her heart, her Pyramus lying there.

Who could describe how her face changed, and how she tore at her hair, to see this sight? She began to torment herself; she fainted, then filled her lover's wound with tears. She played with his blood as she lamented, smeared it on herself, and embraced his body. This was woeful indeed! She kissed his cold, frosty mouth and cried out, 'Who could have done this? Oh speak, my Pyramus! You know me – I am your Thisbe,' she added, and lifted up his head.

Now Pyramus was not quite dead, and when he heard Thisbe's name he raised his heavy eyes to look on her face, then gave up the ghost. Thisbe stood up, saw her wimple, the empty sheath of Pyramus's sword, and the sword itself, that had killed him. Then she spoke: 'My woeful hand is strong enough to do the same as he has done,' she said. 'Love will give me strength and courage to make a big enough wound, I think.

'I will follow you into death,' she added. 'Only death could part the two of us, but it shall *not* part us: I will follow you! And as for you, our wretched fathers,' she went on, 'we, that were your children, beg you to put aside your hatred, and bury us both in the same grave, since love has brought us to this pitiful end! And I wish,' she begged, 'that God would send every true lover better luck than Pyramus and Thisbe have had; and not let any gentlewoman put herself in danger as I have!

'And God forbid,' she concluded, 'that women should not continue to be as true in love as men. For my part, I will prove that we are just as faithful!' With that, she took his sword, that was still hot from her lover's blood, and smote herself to the heart. So, thus are Pyramus and Thisbe gone. In all my books, I have found few men as faithful as this Pyramus, which is why I have told his story. It is unusual to come across such a man, but here we can see that a woman can be just as brave and decisive.

Dido

Glory and honour be to your name, Mantuan Virgil! You go before, and I try my best to follow your lantern. I aim to tell the story of how Aeneas betrayed Dido, and I will make use of your *Aeneid*, and also the works of Naso.

Troy was brought to destruction by the cunning of the Greeks, particularly of Sinon, and the Trojan horse, that was supposedly an offering for Minerva. Thanks to them, many Trojans were killed. Hector appeared, though he was dead, and an angry, uncontrollable fire spread throughout Ilium, which was the chief citadel of the town.

The whole country was brought low, and King Priam was reduced to nothing. Venus ordered Aeneas to fly the city, taking his son Ascanius by the hand, and carrying his father, Anchises, on his back. His wife Creusa followed on behind, and he had great trouble, finding his friends. When he found them at last, he made them ready and, as destiny dictated, they sailed for Italy.

I do not intend to recount Aeneas' adventures on the sea, as that is not my subject: I aim to tell the story of Aeneas and Dido right to the end, as I said. He sailed so long on the salty sea that he at last arrived at Libya with his navy of seven ships. He was glad to see land, as he had reached it with great difficulty, and had been badly shaken by a storm. When they had gained a harbour, Aeneas chose, from all his company, a knight called Achates to go with him and spy out the country. They set off together, without any guide, leaving their ships to ride at anchor.

Aeneas wandered in the wilderness for a long time, until he met a young huntress. She had a bow and arrows, and wore a short skirt that stopped at the knee; yet she was the fairest creature that nature had ever formed. She greeted Aeneas and Achates and asked them, 'Have you seen any of my sisters on your walk? They'd be all tucked up like me, with bows and arrows in cases; probably following a wild boar or some other beast?'

'No, truly, lady, we have not,' Aeneas replied, 'but it seems to me that you are so beautiful that you can't be an earthly woman. I think you must be Phoebus' sister? If you are a goddess, as I suspect, please have mercy on our labours and our misery.'

'I am no goddess, honestly,' she said then. 'In this country, virgins are always walking about like this, with bows and arrows. This is the kingdom of Libya: Dido is our queen.' She went on to explain, briefly, why Dido was there at all, which I will not set down here: it would just be a waste of time. The fact is that it was Venus, his own mother, who was talking to Aeneas, and she bade him proceed to Carthage. With that, she vanished. I could follow Virgil word for word at this point, but it would take too long.

Now Carthage had been founded by Dido, who had once been the wife of Sichaeus. She was fairer than the bright sun, and she reigned over her city with such great honour that she was held to be the flower of all queens. Her nobleness, her generosity and her beauty meant that it did any man good to see her. Kings and lords desired her, because her looks had set the world on fire. Everybody regarded her with respect.

When Aeneas reached the city, he secretly made his way to the main temple, where Dido was at prayer. The book says that at this point Venus made him invisible: I can't comment on whether such a thing is possible. Aeneas and Achates explored the whole temple, and at last they found the story of how Troy had been destroyed, painted on a wall. 'I wish I had never been born!' cried Aeneas. 'The whole world knows how we have been shamed, and now it is being painted everywhere! Once we were prosperous, but now we are so cruelly slandered that I don't think I care to live any more!'

With that, Aeneas burst into tears. He wept so tenderly that it was pitiful to see. Meanwhile this fresh lady, the queen of the city, stood in the temple in all her rich royal dignity. She looked young, fair and lusty, and her eyes glowed with pleasure. If God himself, who made the heavens and the earth, had decided to take a lover, he could hardly do better than this lady: she was so beautiful, truthful, seemly and good. There was no woman who would suit God half so well.

Now Fortune rules the whole world, and now she brought on events that were both strange and unprecedented. Aeneas's whole company, the men who had been lost with him in the wide ocean, now arrived at a place that was not far from the city. The greatest lords among them had split off and wandered into the city, and arrived at the same temple, to find the queen and ask for her help – such was her reputation for good deeds. When they had told her what a hard time they had had of it, what with the storm and everything, Aeneas appeared to the queen, and everybody recognised him. His followers were overjoyed to see him – they had found their lord, their governor!

The queen noted the honour his friends showed Aeneas, whom she had heard of before. In her heart, she felt sad that such a noble man had been cut off from his inheritance, as he had. And she did not fail to notice that the man looked like a knight, and was sufficiently strong and handsome. He seemed like a gentleman, who had a noble face and could speak well, and had good bones and muscles. These good looks he had inherited from his mother, Venus, which meant that no other man was half as fair as he was, I guess. In any case, he looked like a worthy lord.

It helped that Aeneas was someone Dido had never seen before: for some people, something new is always sweeter. Soon her heart began to take pity on his sufferings, and pity began to grow into love. She decided, out of pity and a sense of his station in life, that his sufferings should be ended. She told him that she was truly sorry that he had had such a hard time. She spoke the following like a friend.

'Are you not the son of Venus and Anchises? In good faith, I will help you and show you as much respect as I can! I will save your ships and their crews,' she added, and spoke many more gentle words. She also commanded her messengers to go to Aeneas' ships that very day, with victuals. She sent many beasts down to the ships, as well as wine. Then she sped off to her palace, with Aeneas in tow. There she put on a great feast; but why should I describe it? Suffice it to say, Aeneas was never so contented in his life. The banquet was replete with rich delicacies; the instruments played, and there was singing, happiness and yes, amorous looks.

Aeneas found that he had come into paradise, out of the mouth of hell. His new joy reminded him of the life he had once lived back in Troy. After dinner, he was led into magnificent dancing-chambers, with luxurious beds and ornaments. When he had sat with the queen a long time, and the spices had been taken away, and the wine finished, he and all his folk were escorted to their own suite of rooms, to rest and relax, or do whatever they liked.

There was nothing Dido would not give as a gift to Aeneas, whether it was a fine courser with an excellent bridle, or a steed bred up to jousting, or a big, comfortable palfrey, that was easy to ride. She gave him jewels fretted full of rich stones, heavy sacks of gold, rubies that shone in the night, and noble falcons, trained to hunt herons. Among her gifts were also hounds suitable to hunt harts, or wild boar, or deer, and cups of gold full of florins new-struck in Libya. Dido sent Aeneas all these things and more, and reimbursed him for any money he spent himself. Truly, her guests could say that she out-did everyone in generosity.

Aeneas sent Achates down to the ships to fetch his young son Ascanius, and also some fine treasures such as a sceptre, clothes, brooches and rings. Some of these were for Aeneas to wear: others he intended to give to Dido, who had sent him so many noble things. Aeneas also instructed his son in how to present these things to the queen. When Achates returned, Aeneas was keen to see his son Ascanius, but, as our author tells us, it was not really Ascanius who came along with Achates. Cupid, the god of love and the worshipper of Aeneas' heavenly mother, had made himself look like the child. He did this to make Dido enamoured of Aeneas. That's what it says in the book, but frankly I don't believe it! The fact is, though, that the queen greeted this child so warmly that it was wonderful to see, and she repeatedly thanked Ascanius for the presents he had brought from his father.

In this way, Dido enjoyed herself with the lusty newcomers from Troy. She asked Aeneas about his deeds, and learned the story of Troy. All day the pair chatted and enjoyed themselves, and this bred a fire in the queen's heart. Soon Dido was helplessly attracted to Aeneas, her new guest. She lost her health and her colour. But now we come to the effect of all this, the fruit of it, and why I began to tell this story.

So, it happened that one night, when the moon had risen, this noble queen went to bed, but felt ill, and began to torment herself. She could not sleep, but wallowed in her bed and kept starting up, as I have heard that these lovers do. At last, she went to visit her sister Anne, and told her all her sorrows.

'Now, dear sister Anne,' she said, 'what can it be that terrifies me in my dreams? This Trojan occupies my thoughts, because I think he is so well-made, and likely to be a real man, who knows good when he sees it, and all my love, and my life – they're all his! Haven't you heard him tell the story of his adventures? Ann, if you think it's a good idea, I would love to be his wife! That is all I can say: my life, my death, they are all in his hands.'

Her sister Anne wanted to protect Dido, and counselled her to take care, but their conversation was too long a sermon to set down here. The upshot was, Dido could not resist Aeneas – nothing can get in the way of love!

Next day, when the dawn rose out of the sea, the amorous queen ordered her people to prepare the nets and the broad, keen spears: she planned to go hunting; this is how her happy misery took her. The hounds were brought to her court, and her young knights appeared, riding on swift coursers. These were followed by a huge crush of women. Dido herself sat on a fat palfrey, white as paper, on a red saddle. The saddle was delightfully embroidered with embossed gold bars, and the queen wore gold and precious jewels. She was as fair as the morning sun, that heals the sickness and sorrows of the night.

Aeneas sat on a courser that pranced and leapt like fire. The beast was so responsive, he could be turned with the thinnest bridle. The hero was so fresh and fine that he looked like Phoebus himself. He governed his horse with a foamy bridle and a bit of pure gold. And so the pair rode out together, the noble queen and her Trojan.

The hunt soon found a herd of harts, and there was much shouting: 'Hey! Ride faster! Use your spurs! No! Let it go by!' One cried out, 'I wish there was a lion – then I could spear him!' Thus said these young folk, while they slaughtered the harts to their hearts' content.

While all this was going on, the heavens began to rumble. The noise was grisly, and soon down came the rain, hail and sleet. The sky seemed to burst into flame, and the noble queen and her followers were quite aghast. They fled in various directions: Dido herself found a little cave, where she was soon joined by Aeneas. I don't know if any more people squeezed into their cave: the author doesn't mention it.

There in the cave, the mutual affection of these two began to deepen. This was the first morning of their happiness, but also the beginning of their sorrow. There Aeneas knelt down and revealed the sorrows of his heart. He swore a deep oath to be true to Dido, through thick and thin, and never throw her over for somebody new. False lovers can plead so well that Dido felt sorry for the hero, and took him for her husband, intending to stay with him for the rest of her life. When the storm ended, they emerged from their cave, wreathed in smiles, and went home.

Soon rumours began to spread about how Aeneas had joined the queen in her cave, and how they had done what they liked in there. When King Iarbas heard about this, his sorrow and his distress were truly pitiful to hear. He had always loved Dido, and had wooed her in the past, hoping to make her his wife. In love, we often find someone laughing at someone else's woe, and now Aeneas laughed and was joyful, and lived a better life than he had ever enjoyed in Troy.

Oh helpless women, full of innocence, pity, truth and conscience; why do you trust men so much? Why do you pity their feigned distress, when there are such old examples to warn you off? Do you not see how they are all liars? Where have you ever seen one man who has not left his lover, or been unkind, or done her some mischief, and gone on to boast about it?

You can both see and read about it. Look at this great gentleman, this Trojan, who has such skill in pleasing a woman. Look how he pretends to be so true and obedient, so noble and discreet. See how well he seems to serve her, at feasts and dances, and when he escorts her to the temple, and back home again. See how he fasts until he has seen his lady, and shows I know not how many other signs of devotion. He would make up songs for her as well, and joust and do feats of arms in her name, and send her letters, brooches, rings and other tokens.

Once he had nearly died of hunger, and been in danger from the perils of the ocean. He had been a desolate refugee, and he and his crew had been driven here and there by a tempest. Now Dido had given both her body and her realm into his hands, though she might have been queen of somewhere other than

Carthage, and lived in joy enough. What more proof do you need?

Aeneas was soon tired of deceiving Dido, though he had sworn so deeply to love her. All the heat had gone out of his passion. Secretly, he began to ready his ships, planning to steal away by night. The queen was suspicious, and thought that something was amiss. When they were in bed together, he seemed unwell, and she asked him what was wrong. 'Tell me, dear heart,' she said.

'Tonight my father's ghost has tormented me in my sleep,' he said, and added, 'Mercury visited me too, and gave me a message. I have to sail soon, if I am to conquer Italy: it is my destiny. But truly, it breaks my heart!' With that, he cried false tears, and took Dido in his arms.

'Really?' cried Dido; 'is that what you're going to do? Have you not sworn to marry me? Alas! what type of woman will you turn me into? I am a gentlewoman, and a queen! Surely you will not flee from your wife like this? I wish I had never been born! What am I to do?'

In short, this noble queen Dido sought out holy shrines, performed sacrifices, knelt down and cried so much that it is sad to have to tell it. She begged Aeneas to let her be his slave. She fainted and fell at his feet and lay there, her bright gilt hair all dishevelled, and cried out, 'Have mercy! Let me go with you! The lords who live near me will kill me, all because of you! If only you would marry me, as you have promised to do, I will give you leave to slay me with your sword, right here, this evening! At least then I will die as your wife! I am with child – I nourish my child inside me. Show me some mercy! Have pity!'

But nothing that she said had any effect. Aeneas left her sleeping and stole away into the night, back to his company. Then, like a traitor, he set off for the large country of Italy. He left Dido in her pain, and, in Italy, married a woman called Lavinia.

When he stole away to his navy and left Dido sleeping, Aeneas left behind a cloth and his sword, at the head of her bed. When she woke up, she kissed the cloth and said, 'O cloth, if Jupiter allows it, take my soul and free me from my suffering. Truly, I have gone through all the changes of fortune.' In this state, without Aeneas to comfort her, she fainted twenty times. She also complained to her sister Anne, but frankly I don't have the heart to write down what she said.

She asked her sister and her nurse to fetch fire and other things straight away – she said she was going to perform a sacrifice. And when the time was right, she threw herself on the fire, and stabbed herself in the heart with Aeneas' sword.

My author says that before she killed herself, she wrote a letter than began, 'Just like the swan that only starts to sing when he is dying, just so I make my complaint to you, Aeneas. I do not write in the hope of getting you to return – I know too well that that would be in vain, since the gods are against me. But since you have made me lose my good name,' she went on, 'I may as well waste a word or two on you, though such a course won't do me any good. Truly, your loyalty blew away in the wind, like your ship.' (If you would like to read the whole of this letter, you will find it in Ovid.)

Hypsipyle and Medea

Hypsipyle

Duke Jason, you are a monument to false lovers! You were a baffler and sly devourer of gentlewomen! You set your traps for these tender creatures. You used your stately appearance, your pleasant words, your lies, your politeness, your feigned humility and your counterfeited sufferings. Where others deceived just one, you deceived two! Oh, you often swore that you would perish for love, but the only illness you ever had was lust, which you called love.

As I live, I swear that I will make your name and your tricks notorious in English. Have at thee, Jason – now my horn is blown! But certainly, it is painful to reflect on how these false lovers scheme. Often, they have a better time of it than those who have made sacrifices for love, or endured hard knocks for it. The capon tastes just as tender to the fox who stole it, as it would have to the good man who paid for it. Although the man has a right to the bird, still the midnight fox steals it away. Here

I am comparing Jason to a thieving fox, because of his treatment of Hypsipyle and Queen Medea.

Now, Guido tells us that in Thessaly lived a king called Peleus, who had an older brother called Aeson. When Aeson became too old even to walk, he gave Peleus all his power, and made him king in his place. Jason was the son of Aeson, and in those days there was no other knight who was so famous for good breeding, generosity, strength and lustiness. After his father Aeson died, Jason continued to make such a good impression that nobody wanted to be his enemy. On the contrary, everyone honoured him, and enjoyed being in his company.

Jason's popularity made his uncle very jealous. He began to suspect that Jason might rise so high that the lords of the region would conspire with his nephew to overthrow him, King Peleus. At night, Peleus dreamed up a plan to destroy Jason without any blame attaching to himself. He determined to send his nephew abroad to meet his death. This was his plan, but at the same time he took great pains to show Jason a friendly face, so that none of his lords would suspect him.

At about this time, news began to spread about a place called Colchis, east of Troy, where there was a ram with a golden fleece. There were eye-witness accounts, and rumour had it that the fleece shone so brightly that it was the most amazing sight in the world. The story ran that the creature was always guarded by a dragon, and by two bulls made of brass, that spat fire. The dragon and the bulls were just three of the many wonders associated with the ram.

People said that the island was ruled by a king called Aeëtes, and that anyone who wanted to take the golden fleece would have to fight both the bulls and the dragon. These stories gave King Peleus an idea: he would try to persuade Jason to sail to Colchis, in search of adventure.

'Nephew,' he began, 'I don't know if you'll manage it, but if you were to win this famous treasure, and bring it back here, it would be fantastic, and it would win me a great deal of respect. If you could pull it off, I would feel obliged to do you a big favour in return. Of course, I would be happy to fund the whole expedition myself, and pick out a crew for you. Tell me – are you daring enough to make this voyage?' Jason was young, and had a lusty heart, and he accepted the challenge.

Soon Argus was designing the ships that were needed, and Jason himself picked his companions: among them was the strong-man Hercules. Readers who require a full list of the crew should consult the *Argonauticon* – my tale is already long enough. One crew member, Philoctetes, hoisted the sail when the wind was favourable, and they set out from Thessaly. Jason sailed a long time in the salt sea, until he came to the island of Lemnos. This part of the story does not appear in Guido's version, but it can be found in Ovid's *Heroides*. The queen of the island was a beautiful young lady named Hypsipyle. She was the daughter of the king, Thoas.

Hypsipyle was roaming the island's cliffs, merely for recreation, when she spotted Jason's ship approaching. Out of pure goodness of heart, she happily sent someone down to find out if some stranger had been blown to Lemnos by a storm in the night, and needed help. It was absolutely normal for her to try and help everyone, and generally do good things out of courtesy and generosity.

Her messenger went down, and found Jason and Hercules, who had landed in a boat. They were stretching their legs and taking the air of the fair, temperate morning. The queen's messenger met them and greeted them with due decorum. He asked them if they were shipwrecked, or in any other kind of trouble. Did they need a pilot, or victuals? He assured them that the queen wanted to help them in any way she could.

Jason answered, meekly and quietly, 'I thank my lady heartily, but, truly, we need nothing right now. We're just weary, and came ashore for a change of scene. We'll be off as soon as the wind changes.' By this time, the queen and her companions, who had been roaming all along the cliffs, were down on the shore, and approaching the two strangers and her messenger.

Hercules and Jason realised that this was the queen herself, and they met her with fair greetings. She observed them closely, and could tell by their manner, their clothes, their words and their expressions that they were fine gentlemen. She led the strangers to the castle, treated them with great honour, and asked them about all the hard work and trouble that they had suffered in the salt sea. In this way, and by listening to members of Jason's crew, Hypsipyle learned that her guests were the renowned Jason himself, and the famous Hercules. When she found out that they were also bent on the adventure of the golden fleece, she treated them with even more honour, and spent even more time with them, because they were such worthy folk.

She spent a lot of time with Hercules, whom she thought was wise, serious, faithful and well-advised, unswayed by love and not given to wicked schemes. She unlocked the secrets of her heart to him, and Hercules, for his part, praised Jason until he had raised him to the status of the sun itself. Never, he insisted, had there ever been a man under heaven who was so true in love. This paragon was also wise, hardy, discreet and rich. He exceeded everybody else, alive or dead, in his generosity and enthusiasm. He was also so nobly-born that he was likely to be King of Thessaly before long.

The only problem, Hercules went on, was that he was terrified of love, and too shy to speak out. He would rather murder himself than be known as a man in love. 'I would give my blood and flesh,' he concluded, 'if only I could live to see Jason married. His wife, if he ever gets one, will have a lusty time of it with this lusty knight!'

What Hercules said to Hypsipyle had been agreed with Jason beforehand, as the two men plotted at night. Their plan was to entrap an innocent: to make the queen soppy with love. In furtherance of the plan, Jason acted as coyly as a young virgin, looked pitiful, and said nothing. Meanwhile he gave generous gifts to the queen's counsellors and officers. I wish to God I had the leisure to go into detail on Jason's wooing of Hypsipyle. Suffice it to say, if there are any false lovers around, Jason did just the same as them, with his feigning and his subtle craft. I can say no more – if you want more, read the original version!

The upshot was, that Jason was married to this queen, and gained full control of all her property. He took what he wanted, fathered two children by her, put up his sail and was gone forever. She sent him a letter, which is too long to describe in detail. In it, she reproved him for his lying, and begged him to pity her and their children. Of the kids she said that they were like him in every way, except that there was no deceit in them. She also prayed to God that the woman who had stolen her husband's heart from her would find him untrue as well, and kill their children.

Hypsipyle remained true to Jason all her life. She stayed chaste, and was never happy again. Because of her love for him, she died of a broken heart.

Medea

Jason, this dragon and devourer of love, now came to Colchis. Like matter itself, which always changes into something else, or like a bottomless well, Jason was never satisfied. All he cared about was having his way with gentlewomen – that was the only thing that made him happy. He wandered into Iaconites, the chief city of Colchis, and made contact with Aeëtes, the king of that country. He explained to Aeëtes why he had come to his kingdom, and begged to be allowed to try for the golden fleece. The king assented, and welcomed his guest with great honour. This is how Jason met Medea, Aeëtes' daughter and heir, a wise woman who was more beautiful than any other women ever seen. Her father ordered Medea to keep Jason company, at meals and when he sat in Aeëtes' hall.

Now Jason was handsome, and lordly, and famous, and had a regal look, like a lion. He spoke well, and was sociable, and knew all the art and craft of seduction: he didn't need a book to tell him what to do. It was Medea's bad luck that she began to fall in love with him. 'Jason,' she said, 'as far as I can tell, the task you have taken on is very dangerous. To pull it off, you are going to need my help, unless you want to end up dead. So you'll be pleased to hear that I do want to help you, so that you can survive and return to Thessaly in one piece.'

'My lady,' said Jason in return, 'I am grateful that you are concerned about my safety. You do me great honour, though neither my strength nor my labour have deserved it. May God thank you – I could never thank you enough! I am your man,' he went on, 'and I beg you to help me, because even though I might lose my life, I must try my hand.'

Medea began to set out all the details of the peril he was in, and what he would have to fight, and how only she could protect him, and save his life. At last, they concluded that Jason should marry her, and be her true knight (I thought it best to jump ahead to that bit). First, Jason would come to her room at night and swear by all the gods that he would always be true to her, both night and day, and that he would become her loyal husband, because she had saved his life. And so they met at night, at the time agreed, and he swore his oath, and went to bed with her.

In the morning, he dashed off and put into practice what she had taught him about how to win the golden fleece. He preserved both his honour and his life, and won the name of conqueror, with the help of Medea's magic. As soon as Jason had the fleece, he hurried back to Thessaly with Medea and his hard-won treasure. Her father had no knowledge of her flight with this man, who would later cause her so much trouble. He deserted Medea like a traitor, leaving her with their two children. He was always betraying women in this way. Soon he married his third wife, the daughter of King Creon.

This was the reward Medea got for her devotion and her kindness to Jason. I guess she even loved him better than she loved herself: for him she left her father and her inheritance. As for himself, in those days Jason became notorious as the most faithless lover on earth. In her letter to him, Medea blamed him for his falseness, and asked him, 'Why did I delight so much in your yellow hair, and neglect my own honesty? Why did I fall for your beauty and your youth, and your gracious speech? If you had died at Colchis, many, many lies would have died with you!'

Ovid wrote her letter very well in verse: I cannot set it all down now.

Lucrece

Now I must tell the story of how the Romans rid themselves of kings forever. The tale will include the horrible doings of these monarchs, and of Tarquin, the last king of Rome. Both Ovid and Livy wrote about this, and you can learn all the details from them: I plan to remember and to praise the true and faithful wife Lucrece. Those old pagans commended her for her wifely steadfastness, but not just them. The man who is called, in our legend, the great Augustine, had great compassion for Lucrece, who died in Rome. I will give a short account of her story, touching only on the important points.

When the stern and stout Romans were besieging Ardea, it was a lengthy business, and they seemed to be making little progress. They felt that they were half-idle, and the younger Tarquin, who was a chatter-box, joked, 'We have so little to do, we're about as busy as a lazy wife. But while we're talking about wives,' he went on, 'you should all talk about your own. Praise your own wives, all of you, and ease your hearts.'

A knight called Collatine started up and said, 'You shouldn't go by words, but deeds. I have a wife who, honestly, is praised by everyone who knows her. Come with me to Rome tonight, and you'll see.'

'Suits me,' said Tarquin, and they went to Rome, to Collatine's house, as fast as they could go. They dismounted, and Collatine slipped in with Tarquin unobserved, as there was no porter at the gate. They came to the door of a bed-chamber and looked in. Lucrece sat by her bed all dishevelled, as she suspected nothing evil. According to the book, she was working on some soft wool, to keep herself busy, and servants were working here and there about the room.

She asked the servants, 'Have you heard any news? What are people saying about the siege? I wish the walls would just fall down already! My husband has been away so long, and I am so afraid. Fear stings my heart like a sharp sword, when I think of that town under siege. I pray, God save my lord!' Then she wept, and let fall her work. Her tears flowed meekly, and they became her well. Her honest tears enhanced her wifely chastity: her face reflected the feelings in her heart.

Her husband Collatine came in abruptly, and took her by surprise. 'Do not be afraid, I am here!' he cried, and she rose to meet him, her face beaming. Then she kissed him, as wives do their husbands. But Tarquin, the proud son of the king, had taken good note of Lucrece's beauty: her charming face, her yellow hair, her figure and her manner. Her colour, the way she spoke and the fact that her looks were natural made the prince's heart burn for her like a fire. He was mad with love: he forgot all sense. The fact that she seemed unattainable drove him to despair, but his despair just egged on his attraction. Lust drove out every other desire.

The next morning, when the birds began to sing, Tarquin returned alone to the siege, and walked about on his own, endlessly picturing Lucrece. 'Her hair was like that, her colour was so fresh, that was how she sat, and spoke, and spun her wool. Her face, it was like that; she was so fair, and her manner . . .' thus he muttered to himself, and filled his heart with the idea of Lucrece.

When the storm comes, the sea will shake, and when the storm has subsided, the water will still slap against the shore for a day or two. For Tarquin, Lucrece was like the storm that has passed: he could no longer see her, yet her beauty still haunted him. In his mind, her beauty turned into something evil. 'Whatever she thinks about it, she will be mine,' he said to himself; 'if luck is on his side, a tough man always gets his way. If I plan something, it will happen.'

He strapped on his sword, and set off. He rode alone to Rome, and easily found Collatine's house, since he already knew the way. The sun was down, and all the light had been drained out of the sky. Tarquin slipped in by a secret entrance, and stalked through the house like a thief. Everyone was in bed, and nobody expected treason to enter the place, either by a window or any other way. His sword drawn, Tarquin entered the room where the noble wife lay in bed. As she woke, she felt that her bed was being pressed down.

'What beast is that,' she said, 'that weighs so much?'

'I am Tarquin, the king's son,' he said, 'and if you cry out, or make any noise, or try to wake anyone, by the god that made living men, I will put this sword through your heart!' With that, he clutched her throat and lay the sharp point on her heart. She said nothing – she could not speak. What could she say? Her mind was gone. She could no more complain than the lamb that is seized by the wolf. How could she struggle against a powerful knight? Men know that women have no strength. She could not cry out or break away, when he had her by the throat, and had a sword at her heart.

She begged for mercy, and said all that she could. 'You will get none from me,' he assured her, this cruel man, 'and as Jupiter may save my soul, I will kill your stable-boy, and lay him in your bed, and cry out that I had caught you in the act. Then you will be killed, and your good name will be buried with you.'

Now, these Roman wives were so jealous of their good reputations in those days, and had such a dread of shame, that, fearing that she might lose her life too, Lucrece lost her wits and fell into a faint. She seemed quite dead: you could have struck her on the head or the arm – she would have felt nothing, either good or bad.

Tarquin! Heir to a king, your noble blood should have told you to behave like a true knight and a lord. Why have you trampled chivalry? Why have you committed this crime against such a lady? Alas! This was the act of a villain.

But, back to my story. My source relates what happened after Tarquin had gone. Lucrece summoned her whole family; father, mother, husband, all together, and greeted them in a dishevelled state, with her fine hair straggling down, in the clothes women used to wear in those days to attend the funeral of someone close. She was a sad sight, as she sat there in the hall. Her friends asked her, 'What's wrong? Who died?' but she just sat there weeping. Her shame made her unable to speak, and she was unable to look at anyone.

At length, she found her voice, and told everyone what Tarquin had done to her. It would be impossible to express the shock and horror that everyone felt at that time. Even if those assembled had had hearts of stone, they would have pitied Lucrece, because she was such a true wife. She said that her husband should not lose his good name, because of the shame and guilt that was now attached to her: she would not allow that to happen.

Her friends replied that they forgave her, because it was the right thing to do. They insisted that no guilt attached to her, because she could not have prevented what happened. And they offered many examples to illustrate the point. But all to no avail. 'Be that as it may,' she said, 'there can be no forgiveness for me.' And with that she brought out a knife that she had hidden, and took her own life. As she fell down, she paid close attention to her clothes, and made sure that neither her feet nor anything else would be uncovered as she fell. That is how much she valued truth and purity.

Now the whole of Rome pitied her fate, and Brutus swore by her chaste blood that the whole family of the Tarquins would be driven out of the city. He called the people together, told them her story, and arranged that Lucrece's body should be carried through the town, uncovered on the bier, so that everyone could see the horror of what had been done to her. From that day, Rome never had another king, and Lucrece was revered as a saint, with her own hallowed day, enshrined in law. And so ends her tale, as it is told by Titus.

I have recounted Lucrece's story because her heart was true and unchangeable, and because she was kind and serious. These qualities you may find in women every day: where they commit themselves to love, there their hearts will stick. I know well that Christ himself said truly that throughout the length and breadth of Israel he found nobody who had such strong faith as a woman. As for men, every day you can see their tyranny. Put them to the test, and anyone will find that they are brittle and untrustworthy.

Ariadne

Note – Evidently Chaucer made at least two mistakes in this legend, and glossed over some important parts of the story, hence this note. King Minos of Crete was not a judge in Hades, but his grandfather, also called Minos, was. The poet also tells us that Theseus was imprisoned in Athens – it was actually Crete. In his account of the deadly lottery that selects Athenian boys to be fed to the Minotaur, Chaucer tells us that lots were drawn every year, but also writes that it was every third year. The old accounts differ on this, but most agree that both boys and girls were fed to the beast.

When Ariadne suggests that Theseus marry her, she adds that her sister Phaedra should marry Theseus' son, although Theseus is only twenty-three at this point. Notes in the Riverside Chaucer draw our attention to the fact that in the Middle Ages children were sometimes betrothed very young. Chaucer's 'mistake' here might also be a sly reference to the fact that, though she married Theseus, Phaedra later fell in love with her step-son Hippolytus.

Theseus returns home to Crete to find that his father Aegeus has drowned himself because his son's ship had black sails when it approached Athens. This was a pre-arranged sign indicating that Theseus had been killed by the Minotaur. Theseus should have used white sails: then his father would not have committed suicide out of unbearable grief.

Theseus returns home with Phaedra, having abandoned her sister Ariadne because he judged Phaedra to be better-looking. She may also have been the more intelligent of the sisters, since according to Chaucer she came up with the whole strategy for defeating the Minotaur. Late in his version of the legend, Chaucer seems to forget this, and attributes the whole plan to Ariadne.

Chaucer tells us that the gods were kind to poor abandoned Ariadne. The story usually told is that she was discovered by the god Dionysus, who married her and threw her crown into the sky, where it formed a new constellation.

Near the beginning of Chaucer's account, Scylla, the daughter of King Nisus of Megara (which Chaucer calls Alcathoe) helped Minos win the city by cutting off her father's magic lock of purple hair. She later drowned, though Chaucer only has her drowning in sorrow.

Infernal judge, Minos, King of Crete, now it is your turn! Now you have stepped into the ring, but I will not write this story just for your sake. I will also write it to remind my readers of Theseus' treachery in love, which enraged the gods in heaven, and drove them to seek revenge. Take good note, Minos, and be ashamed. I will begin with you.

Minos was the mighty king of Crete, and had a hundred cities, great and strong, at his command. He sent his son Androgeus to school at Athens, to learn philosophy, but he was murdered there, for no other reason than sheer envy. His father the king was determined to avenge his son's death. He subjected Megara to a long, hard siege, but the walls were strong, and Nisus, the king of the city, was so chivalrous that he was not easy to frighten. He paid little attention to Minos and his army, until one day, when his daughter was standing on the walls. She saw how the siege was going and, when there was some skirmishing, she saw King Minos and immediately fell for him, hard. She found him so beautiful and chivalrous that she thought she might die.

To jump ahead a bit, Nisus' daughter helped Minos win the city, so that it came under his complete control. Now he could decide who should live and who should die, but when he was in charge he forgot how she had helped him, and left her, drowning in sorrow and distress. The gods did not pity her either, but that is a tale too long for me to tell here.

King Minos won Athens, as well as Megara and some other towns. As lord of Athens, Minos demanded that the Athenians give up a number of their own dear children every year, to be killed. This is what happened: Minos possessed an evil beast which was so cruel that it would immediately eat any human being who was brought before it. It was futile for the poor victims to try to defend themselves. Every third year, the Athenians drew lots, and he who drew the short straw had to give his son to Minos, whether he was rich or poor. The boy would be killed straight away if his father did not give him up. These children were fed to the beast.

King Minos delighted in this custom, as he enjoyed avenging the life of his boy, and having the Athenians under his thumb for as long as he lived. After he had won Athens and imposed this annual humiliation on the citizens, he sailed home.

After many years, the lottery chose Theseus, the son of Egeus, the King of Athens. There is no avoiding it – the king must send his own boy to be devoured. This woeful young knight is taken to the palace of King Minos, and thrown into a prison where he is bound with fetters. There he must wait until the time comes for him to be eaten.

You may well weep, woeful Theseus, a king's son, condemned to die so horribly. I should think you would hold yourself bound forever to any person who saved you. If a woman were to help you, I would think that you would be her servant and her true lover forever! But to return to my story.

Theseus had been thrown into the dark, deep cellar of a tower, which adjoined the wall of a toilet. Above this lived the two daughters of King Minos, in large rooms overlooking the main street, where they had a jolly time of it. I don't know how, but as Theseus cried aloud in his anguish through the night, the princesses, who were called Ariadne and Phaedra, heard him as they were standing on the wall, looking at the bright moon (they did not go to bed very early). They felt sorry for the prisoner, a king's son banged up in such a place, waiting to be devoured – they thought it a great pity.

Ariadne said to her sister, 'Phaedra, my dear sister, can you not hear this woeful lord, how he cries out for his family, and laments his situation? Can you not see that he is guiltless? Oh, it is certainly a great shame! If you assent, he shall be helped – let's see what we can do!'

'I am as sorry for him as I ever was for any man,' Phaedra agreed, 'and to help him, I think the best we can do is to quickly summon his gaoler to come and speak to us in secret, and bring his prisoner with him. If he can defeat the monster, then he will be saved – I can see no other way out for him. We

66

need to see what kind of man he is. It may be that if he has a weapon when he confronts the fiend, he will be able to fight it, and save himself.

'You know well,' continued Phaedra, 'that the place where the beast lives is not dark, and it is roomy enough for him to swing an axe, a sword, or a staff or knife. I think, therefore, that he will be able to save himself, if he is truly a man. And we will make balls of wax and tow that Theseus can throw into the beast's throat. These will slake his hunger and also make his teeth stick together. As the beast chokes, Theseus can jump on him and finish him off. The weapons Theseus will use will be hidden in the prison by the gaoler himself, in advance.

'Now, the creature's lair is full of winding ways, just like a maze, but I have thought of a remedy for this. Theseus should unroll a ball of twine as he goes, and follow the twine back out. This will allow him to re-trace his steps. When he emerges, having slain the beast, he should run for his life, with the help of the gaoler. When they reach Theseus's home country, Theseus should make sure that the gaoler becomes a great man there. As the son of a great lord himself, Theseus should be able to arrange this. This is my advice,' Phaedra concluded, 'if Theseus is brave enough to act on it.'

Why should I make a longer sermon of this? The gaoler arrived with his prisoner, and when everything had been agreed, Theseus knelt down and declared, 'You are the right lady of my life. I am a man of sorrows, condemned to death, but from now on, while I live, I will never leave you. If I survive this adventure, I will be your servant for the rest of my life, even if I have to live as an obscure slave. I will forsake my home and my heritage, and serve you faithfully till death, as a page at your court.

'All I ask is food and drink, and for that I will work hard all my days. If you will it, I will hide my identity from Minos and the rest, as none of them have ever actually seen me. I will be so sly that nobody will even suspect who I am. I will change my appearance and my bearing, to bring this off and go undetected by the whole world. All I want is to be near you, since you have helped me so much. I will send this worthy man, your gaoler, to my father. As his reward, he will be made one of the greatest men in our whole country.

'I will dare to say, my bright lady,' Theseus went on, 'that I am the son of a king, and also a knight. If God willed that all three of you were in my country, and I bore you company, you would soon see if I am lying about this! But as I have offered to serve as your page here, I would serve you just as humbly there. If I fail in this, I pray that Mars will be so graceful as to give me a shameful death, and to kill all my friends, or reduce them to poverty. I pray that after my death my spirit will walk the night, and that I will be branded with a traitor's name; which will drive my ghost to walk to and fro, if I swerve from my promise. I hope I will also die in shame if I ever try to be more than a humble page, unless you confer a higher rank on me. Have mercy on me, lady,' Theseus said at last, 'I can say no more.'

Theseus was good-looking, and young, being only twenty-three years old; but anyone who saw his face as he spoke would have wept, for pity of his misery. It was for this reason that Ariadne responded to his offer and his sad face by saying, 'A king's son, and also a knight? To be my lowly servant? God forbid; such a thing would shame all woman-kind! I never want to bring such shame on myself! I hope you will find grace and deep wisdom, to help you slay your foe as a knight should, and

I hope that afterwards you will be so kind to my sister and I that I never regret giving you a chance to live.

'It would be better,' she went on, 'to be your wife, since you were as gently-born as I was, and to have a realm to rule, than to have allowed you to die for no reason, or let you serve as a page. That would not do honour to your family, but then what will men not do out of fear? Now, you know that if I go with you my sister must come too, or she will be killed just as I will. I suggest you marry her to your son, as soon as we reach your home. Swear to do that, and our business will be concluded.'

'I swear, my lady' Theseus replied; 'if I did not, I would deserve to be torn to pieces by the Minotaur tomorrow. I will seal this bargain with my own heart's blood, if you will it. If I had a knife or spear, I would get it out, and swear on it, if that would help you to believe me. By Mars, the chief god of my belief, I swear that if I win my battle, I will not leave this place until you are satisfied that I am telling the truth. But now I must tell you truly that I have loved you for a long time already, though you knew nothing of it. I nursed my love back home in my own country. I desired to see you more than any other living creature. I swear and assure you that I have been your servant for seven years already. But now I have you, and you have me, my dear heart, duchess of Athens!'

The lady smiled to see his steadfastness, his heart-felt words, and his earnest face, and said softly to her sister, 'Now, sister, we are duchesses, you and I, connected to the royal family of Athens, and both likely to be queens at some point. We have saved a king's son from death, which is only right and proper, considering that we are gentlewomen ourselves. That is what we do – we save noble men if we can do it honestly, and if it is their right to be saved. I think that nobody can blame us for doing this, or cast shade on us.'

To cut to the chase, Theseus took his leave, and did everything he had agreed to do, in his meeting with the sisters. His weapon, his ball of twine and everything else was hidden for him, by the gaoler, in the Minotaur's house, right by the door. Theseus was led to his death at the hands of the Minotaur, but did everything Ariadne had suggested, overcame the beast and was his nemesis. He found his way out by following the twine, and secretly made his way to the ship the gaoler had procured for him. This was loaded up with Ariadne's treasure, and Theseus's wife, her sister and the gaoler stole away in the ship, under cover of night. They sailed to the island of Aegina, where Theseus had a friend. There they stayed for a while, and sang and danced, and Theseus took Ariadne in his arms – she who had saved him from death.

When he had acquired a new ship and crew, Theseus took his leave and set a course for home. On the way, they put in at a lonely island in the middle of the wild sea, that was quite uninhabited, except by many wild beasts. They landed and stayed there for half a day: Theseus said he needed to rest there. The sailors followed Theseus's orders, and, in short, when his wife Ariadne was asleep, he took Phaedra's hand and stole away back to the ship, because he found Phaedra better-looking than her sister.

Like a traitor, Theseus stole away while his wife was sleeping, and sailed as fast as he could to his own country (oh that twenty devils would blow him away). At home, he found his father drowned in the sea. I don't want to talk about him any more; I hope that poison will kill all false lovers! Instead I will turn again to Ariadne, who was sleeping deeply out of sheer weariness. She will have a sad awakening! Alas, Ariadne, my heart pities you!

She awoke at dawn, and groped around in the bed, and found nothing. 'Alas that ever I was born!' she cried, 'I am betrayed!' and she began to pull at her hair. She walked barefoot to the shore, and cried out, 'Theseus, my sweet heart! Where are you? I cannot find you! I fear I will be killed by wild beasts!' The hollow rocks threw her words back at her, and she could see nobody, although the moon was still high in the sky. She climbed to the top of a high rock, and saw the ship sailing away. Her heart turned cold, and she cried, 'I find these wild beasts meeker than you!'

Surely, Theseus had committed a great sin, deceiving her like this? She cried out, 'Oh turn back, for pity and shame! Your ship is missing something of yours!' She tied her kerchief to a pole, to make herself more visible, and remind Theseus that she had been left behind. Perhaps then he would come back and find her on the beach. It was all for nothing: Theseus followed his course. She fainted and fell on a stone, then rose up and kissed the foot-prints he had left behind, then began to talk to her bed. 'You have received two,' she said to it, 'you were meant for two, and not for one! Where is the greater part gone? And where shall I go, wretch that I am? If a ship or boat came to rescue me, I dare not go home! What shall I do?'

I need not write down any more of her lamentations: it would be too long and heavy. Naso sets it all out in his epistle, but I will jump to the end. The gods helped Ariadne, out of pity, and in the sign of Taurus you can see her crown shining brightly. Now, I will draw to a close, having shown how this false lover beguiled his true love. The devil take him!

Philomela

You giver of first forms, who made our beautiful world, and bore it in your thought forever, even before the Creation; why did you allow a creature like Tereus to be born? Surely it was not your doing, to make a thing like that. His story slanders all men – he was so false in love and so deceitful. When people say his name, the sound of it corrupts everything between earth and the first heaven. As for myself, I find that what he did was so terrible that when I so much as read his foul story, my eyes grow sore. His venom lingers so long, it even poisons those who just read about him.

He was the lord of Thrace, and related to Mars, the cruel god who carries a bloody spear. With a happy face, he had married King Pandion's beautiful, beloved daughter Procne. She was the flower of her country, but Juno chose not to attend her wedding, and Hymen, the god of marriages, was absent too. The feast was, however, attended by the three furies, with their deadly flaming torches. An owl was also spotted flying around up in the rafters all night, and we all know that owls prophesy misery and bad luck. The wedding celebrations lasted a fortnight, or a little less, but I am already tired of telling this tale, and will pass over the first five years Tereus and Procne lived together as man and wife.

One day Procne began to long for her sister, whom she had not seen for ages. In fact her desire was so strong that she hardly knew how to express it. At last she began to beg her husband, for the love of God, that he must allow her to go and visit her sister, even if it were only once. After that she would return home; or else the sister could come and visit her. Every day, she begged Tereus to send for her, with all the wifely humility of word and expression that she could muster.

Tereus made ready his ships and sailed to Greece himself, to visit his father-in-law. He begged him to let his wife's sister Philomela go with him for a month or two, so that Procne could see her just once more. 'She'll be back with you before you know it,' he promised, 'I will accompany her both ways, and protect her as if she were my own heart's life.'

Old King Pandion began to weep out of sheer tenderness of heart. He was reluctant to let his daughter go, because he loved her more than anything else, but at last he gave her permission to leave. Philomela had begged him, with salt tears in her eyes, to give her leave to go, with her arms wrapped round him, since she longed to see her sister so much.

She was so young and lovely that when Tereus saw her beauty, and her whole matchless appearance, he cast his fiery heart upon her. He was determined to have her, whatever the consequences, and he knelt and prayed to Pandion until the old king said, 'Dear son, you can take my daughter here, though she bears the key to my heart's life. Greet my other daughter, your wife, from me, as best you can, when you get home, and give her leave to come and visit me herself, just once, so that I can see her again before I die.'

Then Pandion laid on a truly sumptuous banquet, and invited all his people, from the greatest to the least. Those who came received wonderful gifts, and joined a big procession, led by the king, down the main street of Athens to the sea. On the way there and back, nobody suspected anything evil. The oars pulled the vessel along at a good speed, and at last it arrived at Thrace. There Tereus quickly led Philomela into a cave, and told her to rest, giving her no choice in the matter. At this, her heart trembled, and she asked, 'Where is my sister, brother Tereus?'

She wept tenderly, grew pale, and quaked with fear, just like a lamb that has been bitten by a wolf, or a dove seized by an eagle, that has escaped from his claws, yet is still terrified, fearing that it will be captured again. That is how Philomela felt, and there was no escape for her. Soon Tereus, the traitor, had taken her maidenhead by force, and against her will. What a terrible thing for a man to do! She cried out loudly for her sister and her father, and screamed, 'Help me, God in heaven!' But there was no help for her, and the false thief did this lady even more harm, cutting out her tongue with his sword, for fear that she should shame him with her words, and show everyone that he was a villain.

He imprisoned her in a castle, planning to keep her there for the rest of her life. She became his property, and he made sure that she could never escape. Oh helpless Philomela! Your heart is broken, God help you! But I must wrap up this story as quickly as I can.

Tereus returned to his wife, and took her in his arms. He wept piteously, and shook his head, and swore that her sister was already dead when he arrived at Athens. Poor Procne's heart broke at the news, and I will leave her in her tears while I return again to her sister.

In her youth, Philomela had learned weaving and embroidery, as women have been wont to do since time began. To put it briefly, she had enough food and drink in her captivity, and as many clothes as she wanted. She could also read, and dictate, but she could not write with a pen. She could, however, *weave* letters, so that, before the end of the year, she had woven the whole story of how she had been brought from Athens in a ship, then trapped in a cave. In fact, her tapestry set out everything that Tereus had done; beautifully woven, with the story at the top of the fabric: everything that had happened because of the love between the two sisters.

Philomela gave one of her rings to a servant, and used sign-language to tell him to take her tapestry to the queen. She also swore to give the servant anything she might get. The servant quickly made his way to the queen, bearing the tapestry, and told her everything he knew. When Procne saw the thing, she was struck dumb with rage and sorrow. She pretended to be setting off on a pilgrimage to the temple of Bacchus, and quickly found her wordless sister, weeping all alone in her castle. Alas, the woeful moans Procne let out when she saw her dumb sister! They hugged each other, and so I leave them in their sorrow.

It's no effort to tell the rest. All I have to say is, that this is how Philomela was treated by this cruel man, though she never did anything to deserve it. This should warn you to beware of men. They may not be guilty of deeds as notorious as those of Tereus, and they may not be villains or murderers, but soon you will discover their true natures. I would say that about any man, even my brother, if it could prevent him from claiming another victim.

Phyllis

We know both by proof and on the authority of great writers that wicked fruit comes from a wicked tree; you can see that for yourself, if you look into it. The reason I raise this is because I am about to tell you about false Demophoön. I have never heard of a worse love-cheat, except for his father, Theseus. All women should pray 'God, by your grace, preserve us from men like him.' Now I will go on with my story.

The city of Troy lay in ruins, and Demophoön sailed back to Athens, to his fine palace, accompanied by a large fleet. On board the many ships were numerous sick, wounded and wretched men: they had all endured the long siege of Troy. A storm of raging winds and lashing rain crept up on Demophoön's fleet, battering the sails. The tempest seemed to hunt them, and they longed for land, but they could not see to navigate, and a wave smashed the rudder of Demophoön's vessel, so they could not steer. Soon the ship was holed below the water-line, and no carpenter could mend it.

Though it was night, the sea burned angrily like a flaming torch, and tossed the ship up and down. But Neptune took pity on them, as did Thetis, Chorus and Triton, and helped them reach land. Of that land, Phyllis was lady and queen. She was the daughter of Lycurgus, and fairer than a flower in the bright sun. When Demophoön reached land, he and his people were weak and weary, and almost dead from hunger. His wise counsellors advised him to try his luck and apply to the queen for help. They even suggested that he should try bartering to get what they needed, since he was nearly dead and could barely breathe. He was dying, there in Rhodope, and he agreed that it might be best for him to go to the royal court for help, while he could still walk.

There, he was treated with respect. He was, after all, the duke and lord of Athens, and the son of Theseus. In his time, Demophoön's renowned father had been considered the greatest man in the whole region. His son resembled him – he had his face and stature; and his falseness in love. It was bred into him: Reynard the son of the fox will do everything his father did, by nature. He did not need to learn it from a book, any more than the drake needs swimming-lessons, when he is caught and carried to water.

Noble Phyllis treated her visitor well, and liked his manner and his behaviour, but I have already written about too many false lovers, and, with God's grace, I need to hurry this legend up! So – you have already heard about how Theseus betrayed Ariadne, who pitied him and saved his life? Well, Demophoön treated Phyllis exactly the same way, walking the same path as his false father Theseus. He swore to Phyllis that he would marry her, and plight his troth to her, and meanwhile helped himself to all the good things she offered him. Soon he helped himself to Phyllis herself, when he had rested and recovered his health. I could give you all the details, if I could be bothered.

He told her he had to return to his own country to get her an appropriate wedding outfit. He left, swearing to her that he would barely pause at home, and return after a month. By this time, he was treated as a lord by Phyllis's people, who showed him all due respect, fitted out his ship, and saw him off with great honour. He never came back. By all accounts, Phyllis took this so badly that she hanged herself with a rope, when she realised that Demophoön had betrayed her.

Before she died, she wrote to him, begging him to return and relieve her agony. I will only give you a word or two of this letter, as I resent having to work too hard to give you an idea of this man. He's not worth a penful of ink: he was false in love, just like his father, and I hope the devil will set both their souls on fire. I will, however, give you some of Phyllis's letter, though it is not much.

'Your hostess,' she wrote, 'Oh Demophoön, your Phyllis of Rhodope, who is so woebegone, must complain to you. We agreed that you would not tarry at Athens, and that you would return after a month. But the moon has hidden her face four times since you left this place, and returned to light the world again, four times. After all that, the Sithonian stream has not brought your ship from Athens, so that it is clear to everyone that I am not complaining any sooner than I should.'

But I cannot give you her whole letter, because it would be too much effort. Her epistle was too long, but I have put what I judged to be the best bits into rhyme.

'Again, your sails have not appeared,' she said, 'and it is certain that there was no truth in your words. But I understand why you do not return: I gave you my love too freely. You have sworn by the gods and betrayed them as well: if their vengeance falls on you, you will not be able to withstand the pain of it. I trusted you too much. I was taken in by your lineage, your fair speech and your false tears. How could you weep so convincingly, just for effect? How could you simulate tears like that?

'If you ever recall what you have done, I hope you will understand that there was little glory in betraying such a helpless virgin. I pray to God, and have often prayed, that this will be the greatest honour and glory that you will ever have, and that if your old ancestors are ever painted, you will be painted alongside them, so that people may see you and say, "Look! There is the flatterer who hurt and betrayed the one who loved him both in thought and deed."

'Certainly, one thing they will read is that you are like your father. I know that he was the one who beguiled Ariadne, just as you beguiled me. In this faithlessness, you are his heir! But, since you have betrayed me so sinfully, you will soon see my body floating into the port of Athens, unburied and without a tomb, hard-hearted man!'

When Phyllis sent off this letter, she already knew how brittle and false Demophoön was, and that is when she ended her own life, alas! That is how great her sorrow was. So, women, beware of your subtle enemy: there are many modern examples of such faithlessness. Trust no man in love, except me.

Hypermnestra

Note: Chaucer seems to have made a mistake at the beginning of his treatment of Hypermnestra, confusing Danaus, the father of many daughters, with Aegyptus, his brother, the father of many sons. The discussion of the influence of Venus, Jupiter and Saturn on the heroine's life, and the feeble influence of Mars at her birth, is an example of Chaucer's use of astrology.

In Greece there were once two brothers. One of them was Danaus, the father of many sons, as such false lovers often are. Among his sons was one whom he loved more than all the rest. When he was born, his father gave him the name Lynceus. Danaus's brother Aegyptus, who was also false in love, was the father of many daughters. Hypermnestra, the youngest of these, was his daughter by his lawful wife. From her birth, the girl was beautiful, like a goddess, or the golden corn in the sheaf, and Destiny had made her compassionate, serious, wise and true as steel, all qualities which became her well.

Venus had given her beauty, but Jupiter lent her conscience, honesty and the dread of shame. For her, wifely honour was happiness indeed. At the time of her birth, the influence of Mars, the red planet, was so feeble that all his malice and cruelty was repressed by Venus. Thanks to the oppression of Venus and other signs, the poisonous influence of Mars was so reduced in her that Hypermnestra dared not wield a knife in malice, even to save her own life. Nevertheless, Saturn had given her some bad aspects, which meant that she was doomed to die in prison, as we shall discover.

Although they were brothers, Danaus and Aegyptus were pleased to arrange a marriage between Lynceus and Hypermnestra (in those days such marriages were permitted). They decided on a day for the wedding, which was agreed to by everybody. Everything was prepared, and the time drew near. In this way, Lynceus wedded the daughter of his father's brother, and she married him.

The torches and lamps burned brightly, and the sacrifices were prepared. The incense burned with a sweet smell, and flowers and leaves were pulled up to make garlands and coronets. The place was full of the sound of minstrelsy, and amorous marriage songs, which is how they did it in those days. All this took place in the palace of Aegyptus, which he ruled just as he liked.

As the day drew to a close, the guests said their goodbyes, and made their way home. Night had come, and the bride was due in bed, but Aegyptus hurried to his own room, and secretly summoned his daughter. When all the guests had gone, Aegyptus smiled at Hypermnestra, and began, 'My true daughter, the treasure of my heart! Since the day I was born, or the day the fatal sisters shaped my doom, nothing has come so near my heart as you, Hypermnestra, my dear daughter!

'Take heed of what your father says to you now,' he went on, 'and live wisely for the rest of your life. But first, daughter, I love you so, that nothing in the world is as dear to me as you.

So I would never advise you to do anything that would cause you harm, for all the good things that lie under the cold moon. Soon you will understand what I mean. I declare that if you do not do as I tell you now, you will die, by the creator of all things. In short, you will not be able to escape out of my palace with your life intact, unless you agree to do as I command. That is what I have to say.'

Hypermnestra lowered her eyes, and trembled like a green aspen leaf. Her colour died, and she looked as if she were made of ashes. She said, 'My lord and father, I will do everything you say, if I have strength enough. God knows I will do it, unless it destroys me!'

'I make no such exceptions,' he insisted, and whipped out a knife, keen as a razor. 'Hide this,' he said, 'so that nobody can see it, and when your husband comes to bed, cut his throat while he sleeps. I have dreamed,' he explained, 'that my nephew shall be the death of me, and I want to make it so that this can never happen. If you refuse, then there'll be an argument between us, by him on whom I have sworn.'

Hypermnestra still had her wits about her, and she consented to this merely to avoid harm and get away from her father. There was nothing else to do. Her father caught up a jug, and told her, 'Give him some of this before he sleeps, and he will sleep as long as you need. That is how strong the opiates and narcotics are. But go to him now, so he doesn't think you're taking too long.'

And so the bride reappeared, with a sober face, as often happens when the lady is a virgin, and she was brought to the bridal chamber with songs and revelry. To cut to the chase, she and Lynceus were soon in bed together, and everybody left them alone. As night deepened, he fell asleep, and

Hypermnestra began to cry tenderly. She rose up and shook with fear, like a branch shaken by Zephyrus. The whole city of Argos was silent, and she felt as cold as any frost. Pity pulled at her, and the fear of death tortured her, so that she fainted away three times.

She staggered about, and looked down at her hands. 'Alas,' she cried, 'will my hands be stained with blood? I am a virgin, and by my nature, by my looks, by my clothing, my hands are not made to handle a knife, at least not to kill a man! What the devil have I got to do with a knife? And will my own throat be cut? Then I will bleed, and be finished! But this business must come to an end somehow, either with his death or mine! But certainly,' she went on, 'since I am his wife, it would be more fitting for me to die honestly, as a good wife, rather than live in shame, as a traitor? Whatever happens,' she concluded, 'he must wake up, and rise and escape out of this window, before day comes.'

She stood over him and wept, so that her tears rained down on his face, and held him in her arms. Then she shook him gently, and when he awoke, she warned him, and he leaped out of the window. He was fast, and light of foot, and ran faster than his wife. She was so weak and helpless that before she had got very far, her cruel father caught her. Alas, Lynceus, why are you so unkind? Why did you not remember her, and take her along with you? When she saw how far away he was, and knew that she could not run so fast, she sat right down and waited till she was captured and thrown into prison.

I have told this tale for one reason . . .

[unfinished]

83

Glossary of Names and Places

Absalom, son of King David in the Old Testament, famed for his good looks.

Achates, faithful friend of Aeneas.

Aeëtes, king of Colchis and father of Medea.

Aegina, Greek island.

Aeson, father of Jason.

Agathon or Agatho, a dramatic writer.

Agenor, father of Europa, who was abducted by Zeus disguised as a bull.

Alcathoe, the citadel of Megara in Greece, besieged by Minos, as recounted in Book VIII of Ovid's *Metamorphoses*.

Anchises, father of Aeneas, whom he rescued from the flames of Troy by carrying him on his back.

Androgeus, son of King Minos, who was killed at Athens, which spurred on his father to attack the Greeks.

Arcite, with Palamon, one of the heroes of Chaucer's *Knight's Tale*.

Ardea, Italian city besieged by the Romans: Tarquin the Proud was among the besiegers.

Argos, city in Greece.

Argonauticon, by Valerius Flaccus, unfinished poem that tells part of the story of Jason and the Argonauts, which Chaucer used as a source.

Argus, builder of Jason's ship the *Argo*.

Ascanius, son of Aeneas.

Austin, St. Augustine of Hippo, fifth-century saint who wrote about Lucretia in his *City of God*.

Bacchus, ancient god of wine.
Boethius, sixth-century Roman philosopher, part of whose *Consolation of Philosophy* was translated by Chaucer.

Canace, ancient Greek princess who is said to have slept with her brother Macareus.
Chorus, a sea-god.
Cybele, Phrygian goddess associated with fertility.
Claudian or Claudianus, Latin poet of the fifth century CE.
Collatinus, husband of Lucretia.

Danaus, father of Lynceus in the legend of Hypermnestra.

Epistles, Ovid's *Heroides*, supposedly letters written by various heroines, some included in Chaucer's *Legend*.

Guido, Guido de Colonna, thirteenth century Italian poet, whose *History of the Destruction of Troy* was an important source for Chaucer.

Hymen, Greek god of marriage.

Iaconites, chief city of Colchis.
Iarbas, king of Getulia in north Africa; unsuccessful suitor for the hand of Dido.

Jovinianus, Jovinian, fourth-century Christian thinker, opposed by St Jerome.

Lemnos, Greek island.

Lycurgus, father of Phyllis. According to Chaucer and his contemporary John Gower. Lycurgus was indeed a king of Thrace, but Skeat insists that Phyllis's father was called Sithon.

Lynceus, bridegroom of Hypermnestra.

Naso, Ovidius Naso, the Latin poet Ovid.

Ninus, king of Babylon, by whose tomb outside the city Pyramus and Thisbe arrange to meet.

Nisus, king of Megara, city besieged by King Minos.

Palamon (see Arcite).

Pandion, king of Athens and father of Procne and Philomela.

Peleus, king of Thessaly and guardian of Jason.

Philoctetes, son of Paeas, pilot of Jason's ship the *Argo*.

Reynard, traditional name for a fox.

Rhodope, ancient name of a mountain-range in Thrace.

Sitheo, husband of Dido.

Sitho, Sithon, king of Thrace, father of Phyllis.

Thrace, area now comprising parts of Bulgaria, Greece and Turkey, on the western coast of the Black Sea.

Valerius Flaccus, first-century Roman poet, author of the *Argonauticon*.

Vincent, Vincent of Beauvais, thirteenth-century compiler of an encyclopaedia of universal knowledge.

Select Bibliography

Ackroyd, Peter: *Chaucer*, Vintage, 2005

Allen-Goss, Lucy M.: *Female Desire in Chaucer's Legend of Good Women*, D.S. Brewer, 2020

Benson, L.D. (ed.): *The Riverside Chaucer*, Oxford, 2008

Boitani, Piero and Mann, Jill (eds.): *The Cambridge Companion to Chaucer*, Cambridge, 2003

Delany, Sheila: *The Naked Text: Chaucer's Legend of Good Women*, University of California Press, 1994

Dillon, Janette: *Geoffrey Chaucer*, Macmillan, 1993

Frank, Robert Worth: *Chaucer and the Legend of Good Women*, Harvard, 1972

Lewis, C.S.: *The Allegory of Love*, Cambridge, 2013

Percival, Florence: *Chaucer's Legendary Good Women*, Cambridge, 1998

Pizan, Christine de: *The Book of the City of Ladies*, Penguin, 1999

Skeat, W.W. (ed.): *Chaucer: The Legend of Good Women*, Oxford, 1998

Skeat, W.W. (ed.): *The Complete Works of Geoffrey Chaucer*, Vol III, Oxford, 1890

For more from the Langley Press, please visit our website at
www.langleypress.co.uk

Printed in Great Britain
by Amazon